Dim Sum for Everyone!

taro

star anise

grater

tapioca

chopsticks

teapot

shrimp

sesame oil

sesame seeds

bok choy

carrots

water chestnuts

rice vinegar

coconut milk

sugar

Dim Sum for Everyone!

Grace Lin

DRAGONFLY BOOKS

NEW YORK

All rights reserved. Published in the United States by Dragonfly Books, an imprint of
Random House Children's Books, a division of Random House, Inc., New York. Originally
published in hardcover in the United States by Alfred A. Knopf, an imprint of Random
House Children's Books, a division of Random House, Inc., New York, in 2001.

Dragonfly Books with the colophon is a registered trademark
of Random House, Inc.

Visit us on the Web! www.randomhouse.com/kids

Educators and librarians, for a variety of teaching tools, visit us at
www.randomhouse.com/teachers

Library of Congress Cataloging-in-Publication Data
Lin, Grace.
Dim sum for everyone! / written and illustrated by Grace Lin.
p.   cm.
Summary: A child describes the various little dishes of dim sum
that she and her family enjoy on a visit to a restaurant in
Chinatown.
ISBN 978-0-375-81082-4 (trade) — ISBN 978-0-375-91082-1
(lib. bdg.) — ISBN 978-0-440-41770-5 (pbk.)
[1. Dim sum—Fiction. 2. Cookery, Chinese—Fiction.]
I. Title.
PZ7.L644 Di 2001 [E]—dc21 00034813

MANUFACTURED IN CHINA
20 19 18 17

To Lissy, who gives my books out at dim sum restaurants

Dim sum has

many little dishes.

Little dishes on carts.

Little dishes on tables.

Ma-Ma picks
little dishes
of sweet pork buns.

Ba-Ba chooses
little dishes
of fried shrimp.

Jie-Jie wants turnip cakes.

Mei-Mei wants
sweet tofu.

I like little egg tarts.

We eat a little

bit of everything.

Everyone eats a

little bit of everything.

Now there are empty little dishes.

Before dim sum became widespread, *yum cha*, or tea drinking, was an important part of Chinese culture. People would visit teahouses after a hard day's labor and socialize with their family members and friends. Teahouses began to serve small dishes of food for customers to snack on while they drank their tea. These small dishes of dumplings, cakes, and buns were called dim sum. Soon dim sum became more popular than the tea!

Dim sum translates many ways. Some translate it as "touches the heart," from "point" (*dim*) and "heart" (*sum*), because customers point and choose whichever dishes their hearts desire. Others believe dim sum means "little heart," because the dishes served are so small.

The dim sum tradition was brought over to the Western world in the mid-19th century. As well as teahouses, we now have busy dim sum restaurants.

There are many little customs of yum cha and dim sum. For instance, when your teapot is empty, leave it open— it's a sign that you need a new pot. To thank the waiter, tap three fingers on the table. And don't worry if the staff doesn't take away your dirty dishes; after your meal is finished, the waiter will count them to calculate your bill!

Families and friends still crowd into dim sum restaurants all over the world. There, amid the rolling trolleys and the bustling atmosphere, people talk, gossip, and share, just as they did so many years ago.

steamed shrimp dumplings
ha gow

crescent dumplings
ham sui gok

stuffed eggplant
yeun ngai guo

fried shrimp
tsi ma ha

coconut pudding cubes
yei tsup go

steamed dumplings
fun gor

sweet tofu
dao fu fai

turnip cakes
lor bak go

rice noodles
cheung fun

sweet pork buns
cha siu bao

steamed meatballs
ngao yuk

thousand-layer cake
tseen tsun go

chicken bundles
gai tsat

almond gelatin
hung yan daofu

sticky rice in lotus leaf
nor my gai

spring rolls
chun guen

pork dumplings
siu my

egg tarts
dan taht

sweet sesame rice balls
jin dui

coconut tapioca
yei tsup sai mailo

stuffed peppers
yeun tsen tsiu

taro dumplings
wu gok